A SARI FOR AMMI

Story by **Mamta Nainy**

Pictures by **Sandhya Prabhat**

amazon**crossing**kids

Previously published as *A Saree for Ammi* by Tulika Publishers in India in 2019. First published in English by Amazon Crossing Kids in collaboration with Amazon Crossing in 2021.

Published by Amazon Crossing Kids, New York, in collaboration with Amazon Crossing.

www.apub.com

Amazon, Amazon Crossing, and all related logos are trademarks of Amazon.com, Inc., or its affiliates.

ISBN-13: 9781542035071 (hardcover)
ISBN-10: 1542035074 (hardcover)

The illustrations were rendered in digital media.

Book design by AndWorld Design
Printed in China

First Edition
10 9 8 7 6 5 4 3 2 1

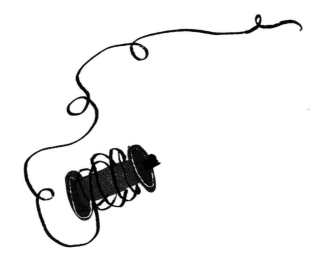

The buffalo have all had a good wash in the village pond and have now gone to sleep.

My sister, Sadaf, is dozing off too.

Abba, my dad, is busy doing what he does
in the afternoons—**dyeing threads.**

And Ammi, my mom, is doing what she does best—
weaving at the loom.

Ammi weaves the most wonderful **saris** in the world, in **pinks** and **yellows** and **greens**, with prints of mangoes, peacocks, birds, leaves, and flowers.

Ammi says that we have been making these saris for a long time. She tells us that long ago, our great-great grandparents used to live in **Mysore**. (I don't know where that is, but I will ask Ammi and tell you later.)

Then one day, the **king of Kota** called many weaver families here. And since then we have been living in our small village in **Kaithoon** in Kota.

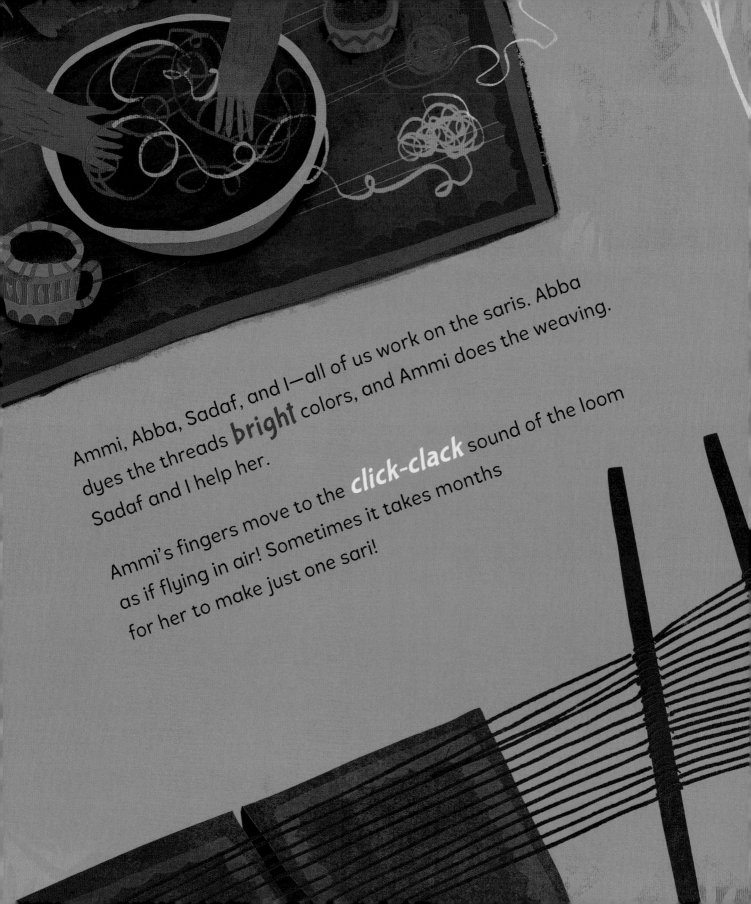

Ammi, Abba, Sadaf, and I—all of us work on the saris. Abba dyes the threads **bright** colors, and Ammi does the weaving. Sadaf and I help her.

Ammi's fingers move to the **click-clack** sound of the loom as if flying in air! Sometimes it takes months for her to make just one sari!

Abba goes to the **haat** to sell the saris. Sometimes Ammi also goes with him.

Ammi makes so many saris, but she doesn't wear any of them.

I only see her wearing old,
worn-out **salwar-kameezes**.

Today Ammi finished a really beautiful sari. I asked her to keep it for herself. But she said it was for selling.

"If we keep the saris, how will we eat?" she told me with a fat frown on her forehead.

Sometimes I don't quite get what Ammi says. We don't **eat** saris, do we?

I want my ammi to wear the saris she makes.
Sadaf always says that can happen only if we buy her
the saris. But how can we? Buying means money . . .
and we don't have very much!

Then I get an idea. I go and shake Sadaf awake.

"Let's break our gullak!" I tell her. "We can use that
money to buy Ammi a sari!"

Sadaf and I have been putting into our gullak all the
loose change that we get when Ammi sends us to
buy anything from the bazaar.

"But what about the list that we've made of all the things we want to buy with the gullak money?" Sadaf asks.

For a long time, Sadaf and I have been thinking of new ways to spend the money while the pile inside the gullak slowly grew. These days when we peep inside, we see a silver glint. The gullak is full!

"What matters more to you: Ammi or 'the things'?"
I ask Sadaf in a grown-up voice.

Sadaf makes a face and mumbles, "Ammi."

We pull out the gullak from under the bed. We go outside and smash it into pieces. The many coins come rushing out.

Sadaf counts the money. But she says it's not enough.

"This money can buy Ammi a towel, not a sari!"

What do we do now? we wonder.

This time Sadaf has an idea. "What if we sell all the old things lying around to Jhammu Kaka, the scrap dealer?"

Sadaf and I collect old paper, empty bottles, and old metal tins lying around the house. We also collect whatever scrap we can find outside.

Then we go to Jhammu Kaka, whose shop is at the far end of the school's street, and sell the junk. We get some more money. Sadaf counts it and sighs. "This money can buy Ammi a **dupatta**, not a sari!"

We take the longer route home, walking through the wheat fields. The dry winds bend the golden wheat ears arranged in neat lines—they always remind me of the worshippers at **Eid** prayers in the village mosque.

While walking, we think hard.

"How about coloring threads for Amina Khala?" I ask
after ten minutes of walking and thinking.

Amina Khala lives in the house next door. She also makes saris, but not as good as Ammi's. She sometimes asks us to color threads for her and gives us some money in return. One time, we also helped her with the weaving of a sari that she needed to finish quickly.

Sadaf and I spend two hours coloring threads for Amina Khala. "Good work, girls!" she says, and presses some money into our hands.

Sadaf adds it to the money we already have and then says, "This money is . . ."

Just as my face starts falling, she screams,
"JUST ENOUGH TO BUY AMMI A SARI!"

We both dance off to the haat.

Cycle-rickshaws clatter along the streets.
Shops and shoppers fill the market.

Today Sadaf and I are shoppers too.

From the same shop where Abba sells the saris that Ammi makes, we will be buying a sari for her—a sari that she has made and she can wear!

But when we give
that sari to Ammi,
what will she say?
we wonder . . .

We don't wait long to find out—
and bring the **biggest smile**
to Ammi's face!

The Saris of Kaithoon

This story takes place in Kaithoon, a town in the Kota district of the northern Indian state of Rajasthan. The town is known for its saris, which are made from a local fabric called "kota doria." This fabric is woven in a special process that has been passed down through generations of weavers and often includes gold and silver zari, which are fine metallic threads.

It is believed that the weavers originally came from Mysore (now called Mysuru), a city in India's southwestern Karnataka state, and were brought to Kaithoon by Rao Kishore Singh in the late-seventeenth and early-eighteenth centuries. The majority of the weavers in Kaithoon are part of the Muslim Ansari community, and most are women, like Ammi.

Making the unique kota doria fabric requires skill and a lot of labor—often the whole family is involved. These intricate saris can take a month or more to weave, and each one is a unique work of art that can be treasured for years to come.

Glossary

Abba: Father

Ammi: Mother

cycle-rickshaw: A two- or three-wheeled passenger cart, pulled by a driver or cyclist

dupatta: A traditional long scarf or shawl for women that goes around the head or neck

gullak: Piggy bank

haat: An open-air market and bazaar

salwar-kameez: A traditional outfit worn by men and women that includes loose trousers and a long shirt or tunic. For women, a dupatta may be included.

sari: A traditional garment for women that consists of a long piece of unstitched fabric that is draped around in soft folds. Saris are typically worn by women in India, Bangladesh, Sri Lanka, Pakistan, and Nepal. Some saris are for special occasions, while others are for everyday use. Millions of women around the world wear a sari every day.